Trials and Tribulations of a Middle Child

Trials and Tribulations of a Middle Child

By
CHRISTOPHER LYONS

authorHOUSE®

AuthorHouse™
1663 Liberty Drive
Bloomington, IN 47403
www.authorhouse.com
Phone: 1 (800) 839-8640

Published by AuthorHouse 11/06/2015

ISBN: 978-1-5049-6093-9 (sc)
ISBN: 978-1-5049-6094-6(e)

Thank You

I want to start off by saying Thank You all for being my Therapists. This book is my therapy sessions at their best. I will leave all interpretations to the reader as to what is real and what is fiction.

My life is full of ups and downs. Sometimes I feel like I am trapped in an amusement park after hours and no one will cut off the rides. I am married to a beautiful woman and have 2 wonderful kids. I work two jobs and got put back on high blood pressure medicine. Yes, I said back on blood pressure medicine- like once was not enough. You would think I would have learned my lesson the first time. Let me take a step back and give a history lesson on how and why I am on medication and in need of therapy.

Session 1

I grew up in a suburb of Cleveland Ohio with my mom and pops. I have an older brother named Brandon, he is 6 years older. I also have an older sister named Stacy and a younger brother named Andy, we are 9 years apart.

Growing up with Brandon was so much fun but I think I saw way too much in my younger years. The best memory I have was playing street football at the playground with Brandon and his friends. Imagine an 11 year old playing football with 16 and 17 year olds. I came home many times bloody, limping and hurt… but I was happy. Moms was not!! Brandon used to get yelled at every time we walked through the door. The older kids used to call me "Baby Shambles". I don't know what it meant- so I did not ask.

One day Brandon got the worst spanking from Moms I have ever seen. Not sure what he did but he received the dreaded **3 MINUTE SPANKING**. One evening moms started yelling at Brandon something fierce. She left out of the room and came back with the thickest belt I ever seen. Brandon had to pull his pants down and Moms tore his butt up. Then she said "I will be back in a 1 minute." Moms went down stairs are started cooking. I went in the bedroom and asked Brandon. "You think she will actually come back?" Then the noise from the kitchen stopped. We both got real silent. We heard foot steps coming up the stairs. I ran to my room. I heard that belt connecting with every swing. I started tearing up just from the sounds. Then I heard that scary phrase: "I will be back in a 1 minute." Once I heard the noise in the kitchen I went to check on Brandon. He tried to act like he was ok for my sake but I knew he was hurting. Oh Shit, the noise stopped from the kitchen. I ran to my room. Here comes the foot steps up the stairs. And there goes the screaming and the smacking from the belt. "I will be back in 1 minute!!!" This time I stayed in my room. This time Brandon started crying and yelling "I won't do it again!!" He started crying while Moms was walking up the stairs. When she got to the bedroom she told him "I know you won't and we will make sure." After this last battle, Moms told both of us that dinner will be ready in 20 minutes. Brandon needed all of the 20 minutes to compose himself. I told myself that I was never going to receive the 3 Minute Spanking.

Brandon was a lot of fun until he left for college. He was there for about a year until my mom took him out. The school called and said he was a no show for classes and was into other things (trying to keep this PG). I remember my mom describing what she saw when she picked Brandon up. My mom got to the campus midday and walked into the dorm room. There were people everywhere, a cloud of smoke was over the room, and beer and liquor bottles were all over the place. My mom kicked everyone out of the room and dragged Brandon home.

Things got crazy after that. I think that's when my eyes were opened to the real world. When Brandon came home from school, he started going out and coming home drunk a lot. I would try to take care of him. Notice I said try. Moms started yelling a lot more now. Brandon's whole attitude had changed. I believe he was trying to make Moms regret bringing him home from college. I stayed at my friends houses for hours just for peace. I remember one time, Brandon was so drunk and came home super late that Moms told him to get out!! He went to sleep in Pops work van. Me being the good supportive brother that I left with him. At about 4 am Moms came out of the house and made us come in. She said," if pops came home and saw someone in his van he would shoot first and ask questions later." I guess Moms still cared.

The funniest time was when Brandon came home about 2 in the morning. He was so drunk that he could barely stand. I tried to get him to bed before Moms woke up. But, when we hit the bottom step Mom came out of her room and started asking Brandon questions. This was the conversation:

Mom: Where have you been?
Brandon: It's only 11.
Mom: Are you crazy coming in this house like that?
Brandon: I don't stink; someone else threw up near me.
Mom: Take your ass to bed and we will discuss this later!!!
Brandon: Ok, I'll take a cheese burger and fries.

I laughed so hard while putting him to bed. I had to take off his shoes and tuck him in. Brandon asked me one question before he passed out. He said, "you think mom noticed I had a couple of beers?" Brandon ended up going into the military soon after. That's when I noticed Pops was a Gangster. I remember one time my Moms and Pops got into a bad argument and Moms called the police. When they got to the house she told them about the guns Pops had. I always thought it was strange how calm he was. The police took almost 10 guns out of the house that day. After they left my Pops looked at me, grinned and said "Yo momma thinks she slick- they didn't take the shotgun in the garage, the two shooter in the bedroom and the 45 on my hip". I just looked at him and thought to myself "Damn – Gangster". Pops was a genius, but he used his powers for evil. At least that is how I saw him. One good example, Moms and Pops got divorced and Moms had to buy Pops out of the house. Well about 3 years later Moms get a notice that her mortgage has been sold to a company name Slip and Slyde Corporation. Moms did not think that anything is wrong. Mortgages get sold all the time. After paying on the loan for about a year Moms asked for an amortization. That is when she noticed that one month $5.00 went to principal, another month $10.00 went to principal and another month $2.00 went to principal. Moms went to here bank and started asking questions. With the help of her Banker and a police detective, guess who was the owner of Slip and Slyde Corporation? **POPS**. After 3 to 6 months of talking to lawyers and with the help of her bank. Moms got the mortgage back to her bank. I know it sounds pretty shady but it was all legal.

I did learn one valuable lesson from my Pops. I learned to have respect for adults. Some people may say that's good, some may say that's horrible. I'll let you be the judge.

I was in the 4th grade when my Aunt died and my mom was pregnant at the time. She had a hospital bed in the family room. I was very upset this day and told the teacher to leave me alone, but she kept pushing and pushing. I eventually snapped and told her to "SHUT UP"!! Well, that was not a good idea. By the time I got home, the school had called and told Pops what happened. I walked in the door and Pops looked at me and said "You want to tell adults to shut up"?! Before I could explain my pants were down and the belt was swinging. The next thing I remember was laying in the hospital bed with whips and bruises on my back, butt and legs. I couldn't walk. My mom came home that night and Brandon told her what happened. When Pops came back home two days later, Moms laid him out. Till this day -40 years later, I still will not tell an adult to shut up. I guess I can say "**Lesson Learned**".

I did learn lessons from Moms as well. I remember one time in particular Moms and I were walking in downtown Cleveland. I was about 10 or 11. We were shopping for some blue jeans. I did not want blue jeans, I wanted a toy. Moms kept telling me to close my mouth and stop bugging her about a toy. Being the hard headed boy, I kept yelping, "I want a toy, I don't want blue jeans." Next thing I remember was Moms stop walking and the back of her hand connected with my mouth. **SMACK**!!! I was in to much shock to cry but my knees got weak and I was looking around for help. All I got was people walking by with that look of "I bet you will shut up now". I became so happy to go shopping for some jeans. I even picked the pair out.

I have to be honest. I did have a little bit of an attitude. Moms used to say I was her mean child. I had a pretty good tolerance for people but when I was fed up. It showed. When I was about 12, my Pops thought putting me in karate class would be good for me. Moms were very much against it. She kept saying I was too mean. Well, I was taking classes and loving it. Until one day a kid in school decided that this was the day to pick on me. I told him to leave me alone and told him not to touch me. He did not listen. Next thing I remember, I was grabbing him flipping him and slamming his face into the desk. After the kid got out of the hospital with stitches right above his eye, my mom took me out of karate class. Even though it was not my fault, I still got punished.

One of the funniest moments I remember is when Moms hit Pops with a frying pan. One morning we heard my mom yelling. She was telling Pops to get up and go to work. Pops went into the bathroom like normal. We heard the water running, so everything seemed normal. My mom must have a six sense or something because she stopped cooking breakfast and came walking up the stairs with a frying pan in hand. She opened the bathroom door and Pops was sleep with his head on the counter. Moms swung and hit his bare back with the frying pan and yelled "Now get in that shower and go to work!!" Pops did so much cussing and fussing but he got in that shower and cussed and fussed all the way out the door. Brandon and I just laughed and laughed.

With the good times, there are always bad. One day when I was around 12 years old, Pops took me and my friend to our first baseball game. It started off the best day of my life. During the 4th inning, Pops told us he would be right back. 6th inning came and went. My friend looked at me and asked "where's your dad"? We started walking around the stadium with no luck. We went to the parking lot in search for the car and it was gone! We had to catch the bus home. I dropped off my friend first, and got home about 11 pm. When I walked in my mom asked "where is your daddy"? I responded with "Ain't he home"? I told her he left in the 4th inning. She laid him out two days later when he got home. He said "I don't see the problem, he's home and fine"!? The sad part is I have never gone to another baseball game since.

I started noticing a lot. One good example, "Ma where's dad?" Pops would leave for days at a time. I never noticed that pops was not at home because Brandon was there every day. The times when Pops was home we would watch M.A.S.H. together. He would eat dinner in the bedroom with a tall glass of milk with ice. Moms never changed her daily routine, whether he was home or not. Moms was a strong woman. She made sure our world never got turned upside down even if hers was.

There was a time when I made some very bad decisions. I had a good friend that was in a gang called Black Gangster Disciples (BGD) and he introduced me to some cool people that were in a gang called the Vice Lords (VL). You would never guess that I met them in church. I guess I clung to them because it felt like I had multiple brothers. Since mine was away overseas. One afternoon we were hanging out at the park and about 10 to 12 kids showed up, in hopes of joining the Vice Lords. They were told that if they make it to the side walk, they were in. The distance was about half the distance of a football field. I watched in amazement of what happened next. These kids started running and then the chaos started or erupted. Bodies began dropping like flies. Kids were getting stomped, kicked and punched and tossed. It looked like pandemonium. After about 20 minutes 5 kids made it to the sidewalk. We gave them much love, because they showed a lot of heart and determination. Or at least that was what I thought back then. What happened to the others, you ask. We left them where they laid. They were in no shape to walk. The friendship with the Vice Lords did not last long because I had 3 dreams that made me turn my life around. The dreams came to me all in one night and back to back.

The first dream: I was floating in mid air looking up and looking down. I could not figure out which way to go. Then I woke up.

The Second dream: Was exactly the same as the first.

The Third dream: I was sitting next to the Devil, having a conversation. He told me if I stayed on the path I was on I would see him very soon.

I woke up and started praying. I cut all ties with the Vice Lords and began focusing on school. I was on a mission to leave Cleveland and go to college. My time is up. See you next week.

Session 2

I want to start off by saying that not all my memories of childhood were bad. I had some really great times. One in particular was when my little brother, Andy, was born. I was in the 4th grade. I was so happy that Andy was here. The worst thing is I was only around for about 8 to 9 years before I left for college. Thinking back all of us were an only child at some point. My older sisters and Brandon are 6 years apart. Brandon and I are 6 years apart and me and Andy are 9 years apart. I figured those were the times Moms and Pops were getting along (EWWWW).

Yeah, I got older sisters, well one sister now. They were twins. There names are Stacy and Tracy. When I was younger Tracy was killed in a love triangle. Her ex boyfriend did not want to let her go. He became a little stalkerish. Tracy finally found a good guy. He owned a diner. One night Tracy was helping her man close up the dinner. They were walking to the car when the ex boyfriend showed up. He shot my sister, her boyfriend and then killed himself. Now Stacy is my only sister.

Moms and Pops got a divorce when Andy was about 3. I still got to visit Pops as much as I wanted. I think I really missed having Pops in the house, even if it was part time. I felt like all the men in my life have left me. Brandon was at college and now Pops lived two blocks down the street. Thank goodness for my next door neighbors. Somehow I kept going over their house and he and his wife became my uncle and aunty. They were the most stable thing in my life. One time I called myself running away and the furthest I got was next door. What shocked me was Moms never looked for me. Come to think of it, she helped me pack. I found out later that my uncle called her and told her I was there. This great time came to an end some years ago, when both my uncle and aunty passed away. I dropped into a month long depression.

I guess I need to reflect on another happy moment… well, even though Pops was down the street, he was only a phone call away.

One time a raccoon got inside the house. Moms called Brandon and I downstairs because the curtains in the living room were swaying back and forth. We made some noise and the raccoon ran downstairs to the family room and hid behind the couch. Moms called Pops for his help and he showed up with a 45 on his hip. Pops leaned over the couch and started talking to the raccoon, "Hey little fella, you are about to die".

As he cocked his 45, Moms started yelling "DON'T YOU SHOOT THAT THING IN MY HOUSE!!" I think Pops was disappointed he couldn't let one off. Moms called some animal control company to capture it. They showed up and set a trap at the front door. As they were trying to coach that thing out. Me, Moms and Brandon were easing up the stairs. That raccoon ran out from behind the coach toward the front door, stopped and doubled back. We all screamed and ran upstairs. I guess all our screaming helped the people trap the raccoon. At least that's what I tell myself, so I don't sound like such a wuss.

Another one of my happier memories was in High School. I was a freshman and had to go through what was called Freshman Day. Now some people may not understand why I call this a happy memory, because Freshman Day is when the upper class whoop the new freshman's asses all day. It's always the first pep rally of the year. All of us freshman were sitting at the bottom of the bleachers and the upper classman were up top. Towards the end of the pep rally the upper classman start stomping there feet and chanting – freshman, freshman... My heart was pounding. I knew this was a right of passage but that did not stop all of us from being scared as hell!! We all started for the gate so we could get to class, but the janitor wouldn't let us leave early. When he did open the gate, we heard "good luck". We ran all day from class to class. Me and my friend had to go to the bathroom about halfway through the day. We tried to go to the bathroom in groups, like that would help. We turned around and 3 upper classmen were standing there. I guess it was nice of them to let us finish before laying the smack down. We tried to fight back but it was pointless. Two to the chest, two to the leg and one in the arm. We came out the bathroom limping but smiling, We made it!! We walked in class and all the other kids were laughing with us because they got caught in the hallway too. When the 3 o'clock bell rang I swear you heard a universal sigh of "We Made It!!!" You could see all the freshmen walking home with their chests poked out and heads up high. We all had stories to tell each other of how we made it through Freshmen Day. Well my time is up. See you next week.

Session 3

It was the spring of 91'. Moms took me to visit Bowling Green State University. That visit meant the world to me. It meant I was close to leaving the nest. While we were on the tour, I noticed there was not a lot of "pepper" on campus. I asked the tour guide what the ratio was on campus. I was talking about salt to pepper. He was talking about girls to guys. He said 6 to 1. I looked and said "6 white people to 1 black person?" Tour guide replied, "No, 6 girls to every 1 guy." I decided at that moment that this was the school for me. He told me and Moms that I could start in the summer. So, I graduated in June and was on campus by July. Being in college was an eye opener. For a moment all my past stresses and irritations were gone. I only had to worry about me.

While at Bowling Green I met some really great people and some questionable people. I learned really fast how to determine the good from the bad. For example, if a person has a "borrowed" urinal from a construction site in their room. Those are the people you should stay away from. If someone asks you and your friend to go and collect money from someone that owed him. Maybe, you should not go. Then you find out he is the campus Bookie. People will show you their true colors if you just be patient. A good example of this was when I was kicking it with a girl. I thought we were just real close friends. Neither I nor she put a label on things. One day I decided to start distancing myself. That did not go over to well with her. She started stalking me;

she would show up to parties and outside my classes. A couple of times she was sitting outside my dorm room. I had to get a little rude. Then a note slides under my door. "If you leave me, I am going to kill myself." What do you do when you get something like that?! I took the note to the head of the dorm. He found help for her. I did not see or hear from her again. I did not talk to another girl for about a month. That situation really messed my head up.

After awhile, I met a really cool girl. She became my best friend. You know my track record. Something wrong had to happen. She invited me to her parent's house for dinner. To put it in perspective – She is white. It is Bowling Green – early 90's. Well she neglected to share that her mom really did not like Black folks. I got to the house and her father and little brother were cool. Her mom barely said 5 words to me. As we sat down to dinner, she placed a bowl of spaghetti noodles on the table, then a separate bowl with the sauce. I sat there confused. I only had seen how my mom and friend's parents make spaghetti. All in one pot with sausage, onions, peppers and hot sauce. My friend leaned over and giggled and told me to mix the two on your plate. Everything was going fine until I asked for some hot sauce. If looks could kill!! Her mom replied with such disdain in her voice, "we don't use hot sauce in this house!" Her dad ended up getting the tobasco sauce for me. I wanted to say that's not the same thing but in fear that her mom would have stabbed me with a fork, I used it with a smile. Again, the night was going good until her little brother used the Tabasco sauce and I swear her mom's head did a 360. She looked at him and said "We don't use that stuff, if they want to do it oh well". I thought about it, I am one person, and then it hit me. OHH THEY. It was time to leave. My friend did a lot of apologizing. I told her, I don't judge people by the actions of others.

We had a very volatile relationship or you could say it was a love/ hate relationship. A good example was one day we got into a real bad argument. I honestly don't remember what it was about but I remember kicking her out of my room and ignoring her for days. Then I got a phone call about 2am asking me to come get her. She was drunk as a skunk and did not trust the people that was their. Me being the nice fool, I got up and walk across campus and brought her back to my room. I finally got her to sleep (at least I thought she was sleep) about 3:30 in the morning. It had to be about a half an hour later I feel movement. When I opened my eyes, what did I see… her climbing up to the top bunk to sleep with my roommate. I lost it. I got up and yanked her down and started going off. She played the drunk card very well. Eventhough I was royally pissed, I did not have the heart to throw a drunk person outside. So I told her get in the bed and go the "F" asleep. She woke up the following morning all refreshed and had no memory on what happened the night before. I made the decision not to bring it up but I did ignore her for a couple of weeks. After I calmed down:

We stayed pretty close friends for a while.

Sometimes in college people make the wrong decision and try things they should not. One weekend Bruce and I was drinking a little and went to a party feeling great. Before we left, we told our friend Pookie not to hang out with some white boys that we knew were trouble. He said over and over he wouldn't. Well, Bruce and I dancing with some pretty females and having the best time until I get a tap on my shoulder. I am being pulled away by someone telling me to go help Pookie. All I am told is that he is in the bathroom. I grab Bruce and we find this fool curled up under the sink screaming they are going to get me!! We knew instantly that he hung out with those white boys and tried acid. After 20 minutes of coaching and pulling, we finally got Pookie out of the bathroom. The walk across campus back to our dorm room would normally take about 20 mins. This night it took us damn near 45 minutes because Pookie kept running from us swinging his arms yelling "They are attacking me"!!!! When we finally got back to our dorm, my and Bruce's buzz was long gone and irritation had set in. We put Pookie to bed and called his girlfriend over to babysit. After going through that, I made a strong decision to leave all drugs alone. Until you see first hand what that stuff does to a person, all I can say is WOW.

Now I said drugs not alcohol. Let me tell you why I rarely drink anymore. One night about 6 of us was drinking in the dorm, having a great time. I decided to try Southern Comfort for the first time. It was great!! It tasted like kool aid. Before I Knew I had drank a bottle and half. Everybody kept saying stop but I was young and dumb and thought I could handle it. Then I stood up. All I remember is falling to the ground and everything going black. Next thing I remember was waking up the next day in my bed with my pajamas on and my friend Marcus sitting in the chair sleep. My trash can had a horrible smell coming form it. I asked Marcus what happened. The first thing he said was thank God you woke up. Ok, this is what I found out. After I blacked out for about 20 minutes, I woke up and started talking about nothing for 15 minutes and blacked out again. I woke up and went to the bathroom and passed out on the bathroom floor. Ohh, after I pissed all over myself and the floor. My friends dragged back to the room and in about a half an hour I woke up and started yelling at everyone over nothing. Then I passed out again. I guess I did this about 2 more times and 1 again in the bathroom. Finally they took me to my room where I started throwing up in a brown paper bag. I threw up so much that I busted the bottom of the bag. Then I finally fell asleep. That was enough to leave alcohol alone. I believe my guardian angels were working over time that night. I straightened up my act real fast.

The next year and a half was pretty interesting and fun. Then one evening my life started down a totally different path. I met my wife to be Susan. Time is up. See you next week.

Session 4

One afternoon I decided to take the trash out. As I walked to the dumpster I passed the sexiest girl. All I could say was hi my name is ...... She said hi back and told me her name was Susan. I could not believe it, I was lost for words. I really thought I blew it. Then about 3 weeks later at a party guess who walked in. I swear it felt like a movie –time stopped, the slow motion began. I was ready now, got my pimp walk on and went up to Susan and said "Hi", with a smile. Thank goodness she started the conversation. Every pimp bone in my body left. For the first time I was a scared black boy from Cleveland. We got along great. I brought her back to my dorm room and ordered dinner. We talked all night long. It was the best night ever. She left the next day back to her college in Dayton. We started calling each other almost every night. Over the next six months I would visit her and she would visit me.

During one visit, Susan came down to chill with me. Just a side note, Susan did not like my best friend. Well, we were in my room and my boy called me and said my best friend just walked in. My inner voice just yelled "Oh Shit". Before I could lock my door she walks in like she owns the place. Melanie sat on the desk with her feet in the chair just talking away. I could see Susan's heat rising. I decided having these two in such close quarters was not a good idea. I suggested we go the lobby (witnesses). As we were walking Susan tries to trip Melanie down the stairs. This was the first time I saw Susan's attitude. It was kind of cute. When the summer came I decided to go to Dayton and work. That summer was so amazing that I transferred to Wright State. I ended up teaching at the YMCA and teaching Multi Cultural Activities at Wright State.

Making the Decision to leave Bowling Green did not sit well with moms. She was highly upset. I had to work and take care of myself. I think the thing I did wrong was start making money. I ended up leaving school and working full time. Susan stayed and got her degree. It was the happiest I've ever been. Susan and I got engaged after about 2 years of dating and got married in 1998. I always told Susan the reason I married her was because she fed me spaghetti. All the older people will understand that statement but for the younger crowd let me explain. This statement is centered around a voodoo rumor on how to get a man to fall in love with you. The rumor states that while making the red sauce the female adds some of her period blood to the sauce and serves with spaghetti. After the man eats the food he will fall in love with the female. I don't know if it is any truth to that story but I have been married for about 18 years now. Things that make you say HMMMM.

As time went on I realized that my life style was soon going to catch up with me. I was eating hot sauce on everything, fast food all the time. Salt here, salt there – grease here, grease there. Then Susan and I got an apartment together. Life became real. We were no longer college students. We were ADULTS with adult problems.

I found out the hard way that I have High Blood Pressure. One Saturday morning I was dropping off our check for rent and when I was heading back to the car I got really dizzy. I started seeing spots. I told myself, just make it to the car to sit down. I remember hitting the wall of the building and then waking up in the parking lot. I sat there for a minute trying to figure out how I got there. Susan convinced me to see the doctor. The doctor told me I needed to cut back on my salt intake and start taking blood pressure medicine. I asked her what the side effects were and she said the most horrible thing. It would slow down my sex drive. Needless to say I did not take them. Thinking back, that was the dumbest decision I ever made. I thought if I start getting a headache, I would sit down and relax and that would take care of everything. This was working for about a year, or so I thought. One fine day I was home for the weekend and started getting a headache. Then the spots showed up. I went to the bathroom and while I was peeing I passed out. My mom found me on the floor with everything hanging out. Most Embarrassing Moment Ever!!!!! After that I started taking my blood pressure meds.

Things were going well but as time went on Susan and I realized we were not making enough money. I was working 2 jobs in the same company and only making 6.33 an hour. Susan got pregnant and we just moved into a one bedroom apartment. Everything was happening all at once. I felt so overwhelmed. I wanted to scream but as I was hitting my lowest point John was born. This was the happiest time of my life.

I have to tell you that watching a child being born was the scariest and most educational moment of my life. Susan was in madddd labor. She was determined to only get a local (this is where the doctor only numbs you from the waist down), at first. But when the contractions really started coming she asked for an epidural. This one doctor came in to administer the epidural. He was just feeling around her back and stuck the needle in. Then said OOPS!! OOPS!! What do you mean OOPS??!! He said there was no scientific way to find the right spot; he had to manually feel for the right spot for the needle. The epidural was working a little too well. Susan was so drugged up that a nurse had to hold one leg and I held the other. Right before the baby came I looked up and the epidural doctor was easing his way around to the front. I said where the hell are you going? I was ready to whoop a doctor's ass. He eased back and looked stupid. Here comes John!! I had my camera ready. Here comes the head – one picture. Here comes the body – two pictures. Look the umbilical cord – 3 pictures. That's when our doctor told me not to take any more pictures or she would shove that camera somewhere. She cleaned John off and showed me my baby boy!!! WHAT THE HELL, HE IS WHITE!!! I had a fit. Now mind you I thought black kids came out black. Yeahh, not my finest moment. The nurse calmed me down and showed me his ear lobes and balls. She told me that his skin will be a beautiful brown and he was very well endowed. I kindly pulled the blanket over my son and said "thank you nurse." I felt a little violated. We brought John home to our one bedroom apartment.

Session 5

Our apartment was sooo little. We were struggling so much. Picture this: Come in the entry door and walk up a flight of stairs. Walk in the front door and stand in the family room. Walk through the family room to the kitchen. The kitchen was big enough for the appliances and a small round table. If you stand in the family room and go to the left is the bedroom. A curtain separated the two rooms. The closet was a decent size. That became Johns' room. You had to go through our bedroom to get to the bathroom. Looking back, John was our Harry Potter.

While living in Dayton I had some pretty interesting jobs. The one that sticks out the most was the last job I had with a well known carpet cleaning company. I had so much fun working with this company. It started off interesting. I went to my interview and the manager asked me one question "If you were single and arrived at a house and the lady of the house opened the door with nothing on but a nighty and propositioned you. What would you do?" Without skipping a beat, I said "I would go in, do my job. Get paid, and then accept the proposition." The manager laughed and gave me the job. He said it was refreshing to get a real answer. The only draw back with this job was you never knew when you were getting off for the day.

I learned very quickly that people live in all types of situations and there are all types of people in this world. One job we went to was in the Projects. The yards didn't have grass. Kids were playing in the dirt. Every building looked rundown. We walked up to the job. A lady opened the door. My mouth gapped open. Nothing but white leather furniture. Glass with gold trim tables. A big screen T.V. This place did not belong in this neighborhood. So I thought. We get to the bedroom, I moved the bed and a bag of weed was lying their. I told the lady about it and her response was "I told my son and his friends not to smoke this in the house." I thought to myself, IN THE HOUSE? So outside is ok? I kept on cleaning. Got to the family room and moved the couch. There lay a gun. Ma'am could you move this? She actually asked me to hand it to her. No ma'am, it's against my religion. Wanted to keep things on a light note.

One house we went to, the husband was talking to us in the living room. A door opened and here came his wife with no clothes on. She stood next to her husband like it was normal. It took every ounce of will power to look only at the husband. He finally told her to put some clothes on. Maybe my sweat gave it away. Another house we were in the owner started smoking weed while we were cleaning the furniture. At least he was polite to offer us some. We both respectfully declined. We both walked out with a contact buzz. None of these houses or people could prepare us for one house, BARBIE'S HOUSE!!!

One sunny morning I get to the office. The crew chief and I get our first job. We get Barbie's house. I instantly pictured a model type. The other crews started giggling. That should have been my first clue. We get to Barbie's house. The house did not look any different from the hundreds of other houses we have seen. Then some kids came rolling by on bicycles singing "Nay Nay you got to go in Barbie's house." That should have been my second clue. I stayed optimistic. We rang the door bell and heard, "come in" from a raspy voice. We opened the door – JESUS, we both stopped dead in our tracks. The smell that came out of the house was so bad; it felt like the devil just two pieced me in the nose. We walked in and stood in one spot. I could not believe what I saw. Barbie was a good 350 lb lady with food stains on her dress, sitting in what look like an old recliner. We started getting the house ready to be cleaned. Then I noticed the stains in the carpet. There were piss and shit stains in the carpet!! The stains started from Barbie's chair to the bedroom and broke off to the bathroom. I could not help but have a look of disgust on my face. I had to hook up the water line to the kitchen sink. OMG – I walked into the kitchen and damn near threw up. There was mold growing in cups on the sink. Roaches were crawling everywhere. Then her husband showed up. He scared the mess out of me. He stood right next me. Oh yeah, he smelt just as bad as the kitchen and looked just as bad. I never hooked up a water line so fast. He said a good 25 words but all I understood was "She don't clean up shit!" I thought to myself, what is wrong with your hands. I went out to the van for fresh air as the crew chief cleaned the carpet. I had to pour Lysol into the tank so the van would not smell. The crew chief finished the carpet and while I was cleaning up he came out and started dry heaving. His eyes were watering and he was cupping his stomach. I got really worried. I kept asking what's wrong? Then he told me. While he was kneeled down getting Barbie's signature for the paperwork. She moved her leg. And he yelled "She was not wearing any underwear!!!" I busted out laughing; he is dry heaving even more. I laughed so hard my side was killing me. As we were leaving all the other crews starting teasing us. My crew chief told our manager that we will never come back to this house. The manager, while laughing, said every crew says that. That's why he gives it to the newest crew every time.

Our couple of years in Dayton were full of struggles and joy. We were nearly evicted twice. Almost had a car repo'd. I was fed up. Something had to change. One weekend we decided to visit one of

Susan's college friends in Columbus. I decided to glance at the help wanted section. Guess what I saw – Taco Bell was hiring at 8.00 an hour! I got so excited. Susan's friend let me stay with them for a month to save up some money and move the family to Columbus. My first job was through a temp service that placed me at Honda. I was so excited to make 9.00 an hour. I was in charge of putting on the emergency brake. Imagine 8 hours a day screwing 5 screws in each car, oh by the way we did 400 cars a day. My right hand was swollen 5 days a week. After a couple of weeks, I was taught how to put the windshield washer fluid in. The powers that be did not tell me not to breathe the fumes. I'm just working along and I started getting chest pains. The lead sent me to the nurse. The nurse let me lay down and 3 hours later when I woke up. I just knew I was fired. I came out of the room and the nurse asked how I was feeling. I told her fine so she sent me back to the line. My lead came up to me and told me – oh yeah when you are spraying the solution on the hoses, don't breathe the fumes in. It causes respiratory problems. I looked at him and asked can I get a mask or something? He said NO, just hold your breathe. Needless to say after a month I quit. I made enough to get a two bedroom apt and move my family to Columbus- Yeahh!!! So I thought.

Let me tell you about our first apartment. When I went to look at the apartment complex –the apartment they showed me was beautiful. The location was great, it was directly behind the mall. But, when we pulled up Sunday with the U-Haul to move in, a guy was in the parking lot yelling and screaming because all his windows were busted out and all his clothes were thrown everywhere. Susan looked at me and said "Where in the Hell did you bring us?!" I just knew she would be happy once we got in the building. Well, we walked into the nastiest looking hallway. It smelt like throw up and looked like someone pissed all over the floor and walls. We got to the 3rd floor and were so happy when we got in the apartment. As time went on we met our neighbor across the hall. She was sweet as pie. Did I mention she was a hooker? Susan was not too happy. Then we found out the people that lived below us were drug dealers. I swear, can a brotha get a break!!!! I was determined to make this work. Susan got a good job working with families and we found a lady to watch John for only 60.00 a week. I got a job as a security guard for a company downtown. I was so happy for the moment. Our family was together we were able to put food on the table. After our year lease was up we decided to rent a house in the Northern Lights area. The house was really nice with a nice size yard. After about 6 months I noticed that the house had a lean to it. We found out it had termites. We could not wait to get out. Then we found a house on 19th and Cleveland. A cute 3 bedroom, 1 bath with a full basement. Nobody told me or educated me on what neighborhood to live in and which ones not to. South Linden should not have been on the list. The next 8 years was pure craziness.

Session 6

We thought we had found a diamond in the ruff. We rented a two bedroom house in South Linden for a year. The first few weeks were quiet. Then we would here a few gun shots here and there. It was never on our street. Susan was about to deliver our second child, Jack. Nothing could break my spirit. I was on cloud 9. Susan had Jack at OSU. He was a C section due to complications. So I could not be in the room. When we brought him home everything was wonderful. We decided to ask Mr. Jones how much he wanted for the house. He said 54,000.00 at first. 2 weeks later he said 42,000.00. It felt like God was negotiating for us. 3 weeks later he came back and said "how about 38,000.00. I just want to pay off my Cadillac." We took it. Home owners – I could not believe it. As time went on we understood why he sold us the house so cheap. One Saturday we were talking to the neighbors and they asked did Mr. Jones tell you what happened to the last owners? They told us the Granddad and Grandson were killed in the attic. Someone he knew came in asking for money. When he did not get what he wanted he shot both of them in the attic. Then, from that moment on every creek and noise we just knew there were ghost.

As the years went on the neighborhood got worst. We were going to bed by gun fire. At least 2 times a week we would hear police cars, ambulance and fire trucks. It's sad when this becomes normal. We ended up getting an Akita. This was my favorite dog we ever had. No matter what was happening Khovu always gave me love. Thinking back, I relied on his love to make it day by day. Things were getting tough with my marriage. I was stressing with my job. I even wrote my own prayer to help me get through. Things were hitting me from all sides that were raising my stress level. One day in Dec. of 99' I had a heart attack. My job was stressing me out so bad. I would argue with my supervisor at least 2 or 3 times a week. One afternoon my chest felt like someone was stabbing me with a butcher knife every time I took a deep breath. I told my boss and he told me to drive myself to the hospital. And then he told me that if I leave it would be an occurrence. I got so mad that I drove to St. Ann's hospital in pain. When I got there, I waited for about an hour taking short breaths. Then finally they got me back and hooked up a couple of sticky things to my chest. Twenty minutes later nurses came running in, putting an IV in my arm and hooking more sticky things to my chest. An older lady grabbed my hand and told me to relax. REALLY!! At this point I was freaking out. I had no idea what was going on. The doctor said they were going to run the test one more time. Fifteen minutes later my bag was put on my chest, I was being wheeled to another room and a Cardiologist was being called. The doctor told me that both test came back as a heat attack. By the time the Cardiologist got there I had relaxed and he ran another test. He told me that the heart attack was stress related and my heart was ok. I had to make some changes in my life. The next week I quit my job and got into the mutual fund industry. The company I started working for, started off wonderful. I made a decision to not let stress control me.

A few years went by and financial problems started creeping up again. I was getting bombarded with family issues and my marriage was turning upside down again! Susan and I were arguing all the time. I got a second job as an assistant manager of a well known video store to get out of the house and bring in more money. As times got harder I pulled out the prayer I wrote a while back:

> Dear Lord,
> I am asking you to guide me
> Guide me with my finances
> Guide me with this car
> Guide me with this Marriage
> Guide my life Lord!!!
> And Lord please give me understanding to know where you are taking me.
> I feel so alone right now
> My boys are to young to understand
> I have to stay strong for them
> My wife has proven and shown to me over and over again that she is not in my corner and has no desire to comfort me when I am down.
> It feels like she enjoys watching me suffer or have pain.
> Lord, Am I reading the wrong signs???
> You are the only one that truly has my back.
> That truly loves me!!!
> I am leaning on your strength Lord, in hopes that it will strengthen me!!
> Thank you for watching over me and keeping me strong to deal with all adversities in my life.
> Love you and Thank you, Lord Amen

Session 7

I worked for a mutual fund company for over 11 years. The last 6 months I worked their was hell and high water. Another co-worker and I started arguing all the time. We would cuss each other out on the floor so much that people stopped looking up. I remember one time I was sitting in my supervisor's cube when this co-worker came up and called me a Bitch. I looked up and called him an Asshole. My supervisor stopped turned around looked at both of us and turned back around and kept on working. He did not say a word. I thought to myself this is ridiculous I cannot keep working in this hostile environment.

On the flip side my job at the video store was wonderful from start to finish. I loved my customers and co-workers. We had a guy that robbed the video store across the street and came to my store to spend the money. We did have one guy try and rob my store. He came in and told the customer service rep. and manager on duty not to move. He was trying to pull the gun out of his pocket but it was wrapped around the extension cord he was going to use to tie up the employees. Since he could not get the gun out he grabbed some candy off the counter and ran out. The fool got on the bus across the street. The cops showed up and the customers told the cops that he was on the bus. The cops stopped the bus from pulling off and arrested the guy. But like all good things, it had to come to an end. I had to leave the job due to the lack of benefits. Then I became a full time Insurance agent. LOVED IT!!!

I met some very interesting people. I remember this couple wanted to talk about life insurance. I hopped in my car and drove two hours to this meeting. I started reviewing the **seven** policies he already had. A couple were good but some preyed on his fears. For example: Get paid 7,000.00 in accidental death insurance but only if you die on a train or a plane. I asked the couple, when was the last time they took a train? There response was never. I asked, how often do you two fly? There response was never. We are scared to fly. With a puzzled look on my face, I asked why you have this insurance. There response, you never know what might happen. I found a Cancer policy that paid $200.00 a day if diagnosed with Cancer but only for 3 mos. The wife told me that if he passes, she was going to wheel his ass on to a plane. What got me nervous was the question of how much for a 3 million dollar policy? I told her and then she asked how long do you have to wait for the insurance not to investigate the death. I reluctantly told her two years. I gave that nervous laugh and looked at the husband. He had this look of desperation. I cut the meeting short and left. For the husbands sake I did not write that policy. Susan kept pressuring me to get a job with a steady paycheck, so I applied at a distribution center. I found out that I am not 18 anymore.

During the interview they told everyone that if you had anything other than a parking ticket you should leave. And if you have done any drugs in the past 6 months you should leave. Three people got up and left. I made it to the 2nd interview. The second interview was a one on one talk. After I accepted they pulled out a swab and stuck it in my mouth. I found out I got the job a week later. I wasn't worried but….. When I finished my three week training. I started at the distribution center. I was so excited. The manager gave me two choices- Produce or Freezer. I chose freezer because the boxes were suppose to be lighter. I quickly found out that the boxes were suppose to lighter but it was **-34** degrees in the freezer!!! I think I found out what Hell would feel like if it was frozen over. I had ice cycles on my mustache, eye lashes and nose hair. I think my balls ran up in my stomach. I did find out that the company lied. I was on break and over heard people talking. One guy said "I don't know how I got hired because I smoked a bowl right before the interview." My eyes got huge. Then another guy said "I know, I just got out of county 3 weeks ago. I thought to myself, "Oh shit, I work with a bunch of drug heads and criminals." While I was working there I was damn near killing myself. This is an example of how a day was for me. Drink two cups of coffee on my way to work. A can of Mt Dew at work before the start of my shift. First break, bottle of water. Lunch time, can of Mt Dew. Second break, can of Monster. End of shift, can of Mt. Dew for the drive home. My piss was a dirty yellow. I swear I felt my liver shriveling up. I started popping pain pills everyday. After three and half months I had to quit.

I finally got a job at my dream company. Things were finally looking up. I am happy with my job. My stress level was going down. It seemed like I really found the silver lining. Then the phone calls started. End of session –AGHH

Session 8

Now you know what my job and financial stresses came from. Other pieces of my stress come from family and marriage. Even though I try to focus on my marriage and family, my brothers and sister issues always keep popping up. My mom likes to call me and tell me everyone's issues. I usually can't help fix other peoples problems but I always try. I think I am her outlet. Because their problems are way too complicated, I stopped asking if I can help. I have gone as far as to not letting my family use my address or phone number. Let me tell you why. Some years ago my wife and I moved out to the suburbs. This city had very little "pepper" in a whole lot of "salt". We had a beautiful half a double in a quiet cul da sac. Back then I let people use my address for mail and packages. My brothers did not trust their neighbors. One day I came home from work and my neighbor stopped me. She asked me if I had a brother or not. I told her yes and asked why. Well, she proceeded to tell me that earlier that day she woke up to banging. When she looked out S.W.A.T. was at my door. They had the whole cul de sac blocked off and was about to knock down my door. She went outside and told them she is not home. They showed her a picture and asked if he lived here. She told them no. She described the picture to me. Once I caught my breath I made a decision. My family cannot use my address ever again.! My wife was so embarrassed. That was a great way to be introduced to a new city. S.W.A.T!!!!

I have learned the hard way that marriage is a roller coaster ride. You have the ups and then it becomes steady and calm then the downs. When you go down, the screaming starts. Susan and I have had plenty of ups and downs during our relationship. When we first met I knew she was the one. My mom told me there are a few test to do to find out if you have a good woman or not.

First one is, when you let her into the car does she just sit there or does she reach over and attempt to open you door? If she just sits there cut ties and leave this girl is selfish. If she reaches over and opens your door she is considerate and is a keeper. Second one is, fart in front of her. If she leaves and complains cut ties. If she stays and farts with you this shows she is comfortable and is willing to let you see all sides of her. Third one is, call her into the bathroom to talk while you are taking a shit. This is the big one. If she does not come close to talk cut ties. She does not want to be around when things are bad. If she comes in and talks to you or better yet calls you into the bathroom to talk while she is on the toilet. This is a girl that will ride or die for you. I tried each of the tests with Susan at different points of our relationship. First one went off without a hitch. The Second was fun until she farted. I struggled to stay but I did. You have to understand it smelt like death. The third did not work the first time. This had me worried. But a few months later I tried again and it went off without a hitch. After 18 years we go to bathroom with the door open. That's a marriage.

One of the best times we had is on weekends we use to go to the hotel (Home Wood Suites). It was our way of getting away from everyone and everything. These weekends really helped us to connect. With all the other stresses going on in my life this was stress free. Sometimes I think that maybe we should have stayed in Dayton where we had less worries. We moved to the big city of Columbus and two kids later major issues and stress started showing up. At one point we almost got divorced. Now when I tell you this story, I understand half of why it happened and the other half I think it is deeper issues going on. You be the judge. When we first met I smoked cigarettes for a few years and I decided to quit. Well I did quite for about 2 years. But I was working at a job and I was bored and everyone around me was smoking so I started back up. I should have discussed it with Susan at that time but like a fool I didn't. I knew she did not like the fact that I smoked so instead of adding gasoline to the fire and have an argument. I kept my smoking a secret for a very long time. Then one day she found my pack in my bag. She went off on me. I thought the devil came out. I became the most horrible person in the world. I was every name you can think of. Well after a few months of living in a hostile environment we tried counseling. When we met with the counselor his first question was "why are we here?" Susan states **HE IS SMOKING!** He asked me what I am smoking, so I told him cigarettes. He told me not to lie and tell him what I was smoking. I told him again "cigarettes". He giggled and said it is deeper issues going on. We went to 3 sessions and nothing was changing and I felt Susan was not trying. So we stopped. At this time we were in agreement to get a dissolution and go our separate ways. Well one day I decided to look up how much child support would cost. After I woke up from shock I told Susan we need to work this out. Well 16 years later I think we made the correct decision.

I guess you are wondering how I have made it this far, GOD! I know I have Angels working overtime on my ass. Even though stress never stops, it does depend on how you deal with it. I have learned to try and learn a lesson from each situation. A lot of time, the lesson I have to learn is not what I want to learn. I do believe my disposition is a product of my past, whether good or bad. Not to mention I am a very paranoid person. It is so bad that if we go out to eat I always (try to) sit with my back to a wall or to the fewest amount of people. Susan always said "You have done and seen too much in your past- now you don't trust anybody." I don't think she knows how right she is. Don't get me wrong, I am a very friendly person. I am a very unorthodox person. As long as I know how you are, we can get along. Well I guess all my free sessions are up. Thank you for letting me vent. This therapy has helped a lot!!! I got a feeling we will hear from each other again.

AGGHH, ANOTHER PHONE CALL..
..............Well, here we go back to therapy.

C.L. 2015

Printed in the United States
By Bookmasters